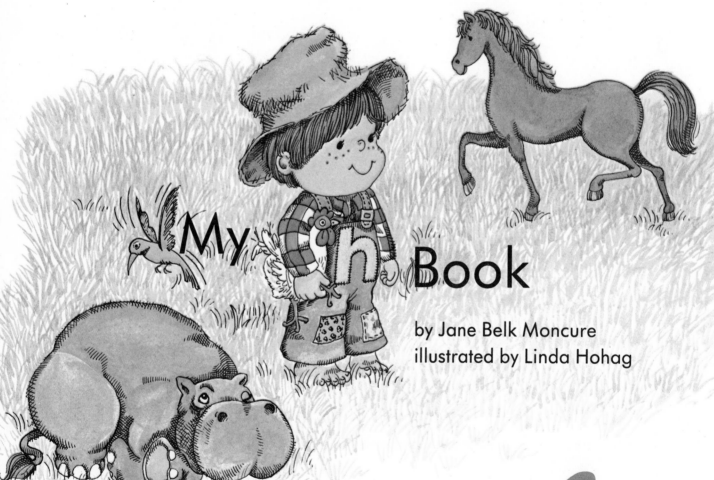

My h Book

by Jane Belk Moncure

illustrated by Linda Hohag

THE CHILD'S WORLD

ELGIN, ILLINOIS 60120

Library of Congress Cataloging in Publication Data

Moncure, Jane Belk.
  My "h" book.

  (My first steps to reading)
  Rev. ed. of: My h sound box. © 1977.
  Summary: Little h has adventures with things
beginning with the letter h.
  1. Children's stories, American. [1. Alphabet]
I. Hohag, Linda. ill. II. Moncure, Jane Belk. My
h sound box. III. Title. IV. Series: Moncure,
Jane Belk. My first steps to reading.
PZ7.M739Myh 1984   [E]   84-17541
ISBN 0-89565-282-X

Distributed by Childrens Press, 1224 West Van Buren Street,
Chicago, Illinois 60607.

My "h" Book

Little h had a box.

He said, "I will fill my box."

He found hats.

He put on a hat.

He put lots
of hats into
his box.

box

Little  h found a hen.

"Hi, hen," he said.
"Come into
my box."

box

Then he found a  hog.

box

Into his box
went the hog!

Little  h found a horse.

He hopped on.

11

The horse
went up the hill.

"Go higher," said Little .

But the horse stopped.
So Little put the horse
into his box.

box

Then he found a

helicopter.

The helicopter could go high.

But the helicopter went too high.

So Little h put it into his box.

Little  put the box on his head.

He did not see the hole.

Down they went.

"How can we get out…

of this hole?"

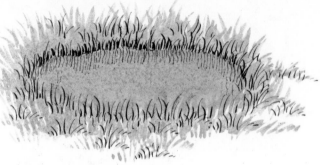

asked
the hen,

the hog,

and the horse.

Little  had a horn.

"I will blow my horn," he said. "Toot, toot."

A hippo heard the horn.

She helped them out of the hole.

"How can I thank you?"

Little  h asked.

"I like your helicopter," said the hippo.

"How about a ride?"

Little  h took the helicopter out of his box.

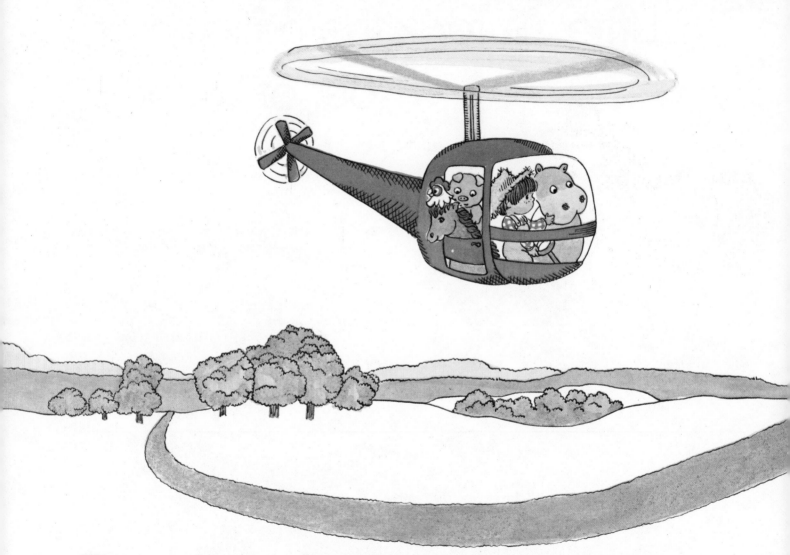

Then they flew up and away...

all the way home.

Little h was happy ...

helicopter

hen

horn

hog

with all his things.

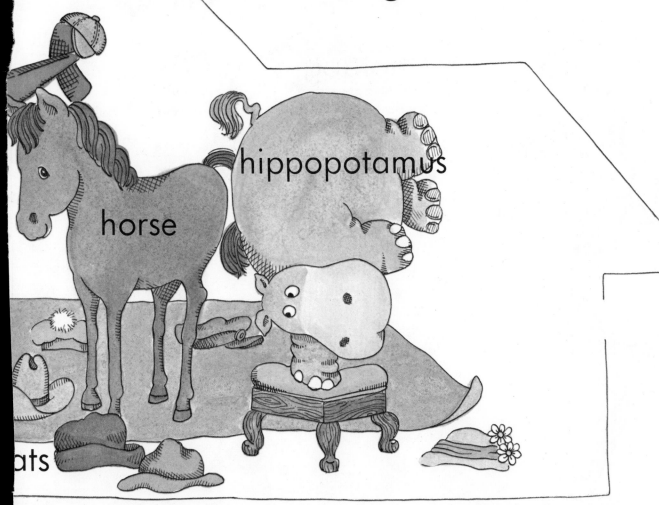

horse

hippopotamus

ats

27

More words with Little

hair

hotdog

harp

hand

honey

28

hummingbird

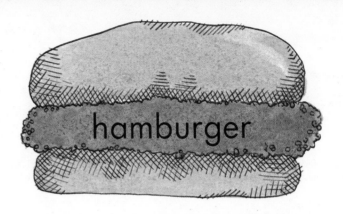

hamburger

hammer

hood

hive

hospital

heart

29